D1533569

Dalmatian Press, LLC, 2006. All Rights Reserved. Printed in China.
The DALMATIAN PRESS name and logo are trademarks of Dalmatian Press, LLC, Franklin, Tennessee 37067.
No part of this book may be reproduced or copied in any form without written permission of Dalmatian Press,
BVS Entertainment, Inc., and BVS International N.V.

06 07 08 09 QPP 10 9 8 7 6 5 4 3 2 1
15680 Power Rangers Handle Box Set Book - Wild Force: Red Lion Roar

This is Animarium—the great floating island, home of Princess Shayla and the Wild Zords, guardians of the power of good.

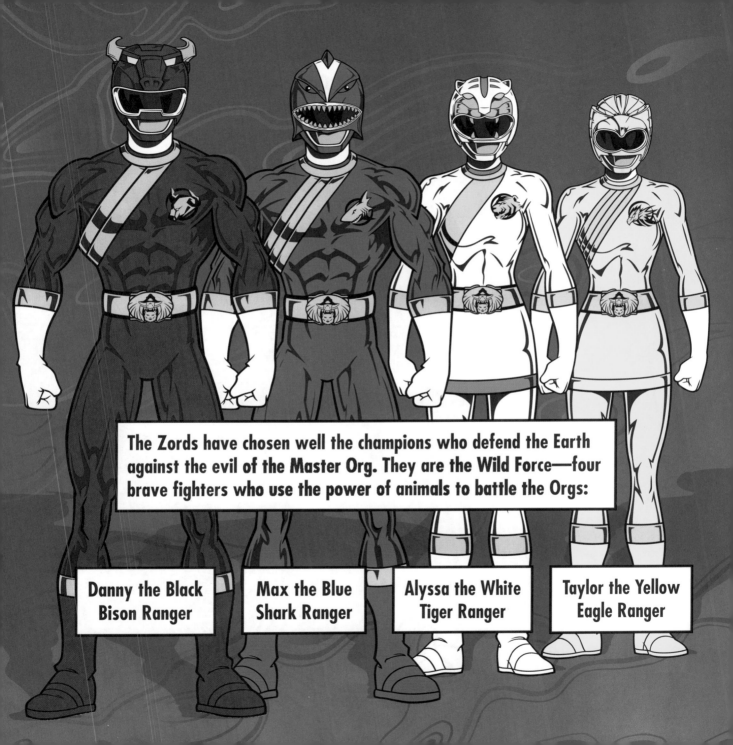

The Zords have chosen well the champions who defend the Earth against the evil of the Master Org. They are the Wild Force—four brave fighters who use the power of animals to battle the Orgs:

Danny the Black Bison Ranger

Max the Blue Shark Ranger

Alyssa the White Tiger Ranger

Taylor the Yellow Eagle Ranger

Back in Animarium, Princess Shayla touched her jeweled neckpiece and spoke to the Rangers. "Rangers, I have found the fifth Ranger. His name is Cole. He has been transported here to Animarium for training. I will send him to join you."

Cole had awakened to a new, amazing world. An Eagle's cry filled the air, and great Animal Zords appeared before him.

Back in the city, people fled from the Turbine and Plugma Orgs.

"Earth belongs to us Orgs!" cried Turbine Org as he fired his sparks around the city. Little did the Org know that the Wild Force had become a team of five....

"It is now time to find out if the Lion chose the right person," said Taylor.

"Just tell me what to do," replied Cole. The four Rangers pulled out their phones—and handed one to Cole. "Wild access!" "Wild access!" repeated Cole. The five morphed into the Wild Force Rangers!

"Let's finish off those Orgs!" commanded Danny.

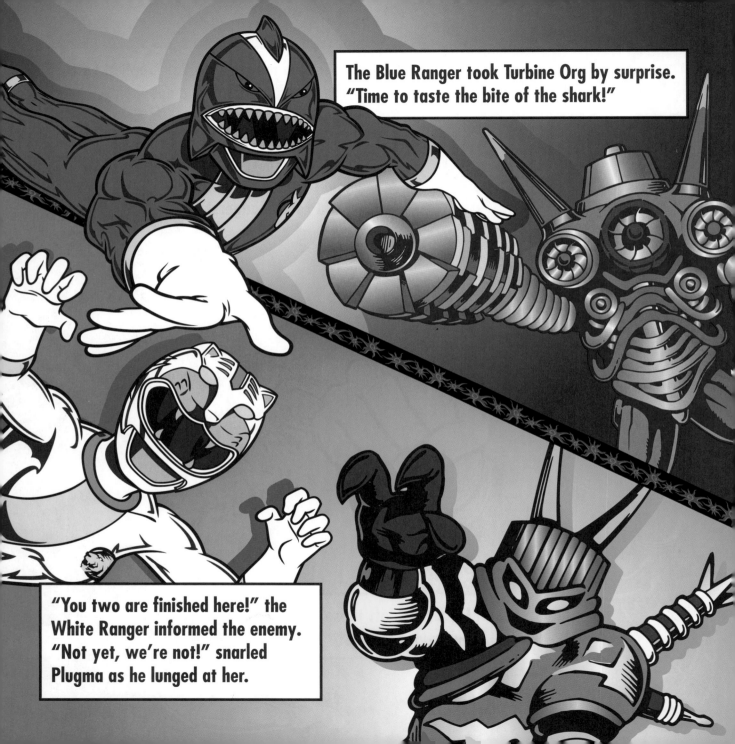

Cole leaped in to help his fellow Ranger. "I think I like this!" he thought. But just then, the Orgs joined arms and sent a **powerful** energy blast that hurled the Rangers into the air.

"Listen to me!" cried Cole. "My Lion patch is telling me that only one can defeat two! I think we have to combine our weapons and work together!"

"Let's do it!" said the Black Bison.
The five Rangers pulled out their weapons—
"Red Lion Fang!"
"Golden Eagle Sword!"
"Blue Shark Fighting Fins!"
"Black Bison Axe!"
"White Tiger Baton!"

As the Sword's mighty beam turned Plugma into a mound of slime, Turbine Org limped to safety and met up with Jindrax and Toxica. "We have a way to help you," said Toxica. With her evil powers, she turned the Org into a Giant Turbine!

"Oh, no! It's impossible!" cried the White Ranger. "Man, that is big!" said the Black Ranger. "The world is mine!" laughed Giant Turbine Org.

From Animarium, Princess Shayla sent a message: "Rangers, the time has come. Put your crystals in your Crystal Sabers and call the Wild Zords down from Animarium!"

The Rangers inserted their crystals and held their sabers high—summoning the Wilds Zords! "Now, Org, you'll feel the full power of the Wild Force!" roared Cole. The Zords attacked Giant Turbine. The monster was stunned—but not stopped!

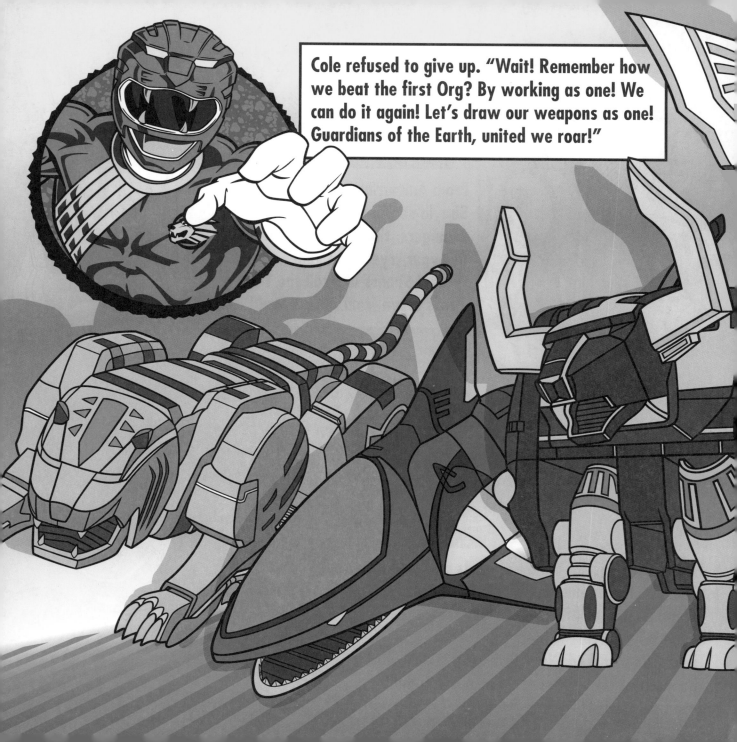

The Rangers held their weapons toward the Giant Turbine and proclaimed:
"Wild Force—Mega-Roar!"

Beams of powerful energy shot out and joined energy beams from the Animal Zords. The incredible blast hit Giant Turbine Org—destroying him—forever!

That night, Jindrax and Toxica cowered together in the shadows.
"My Org! My poor, poor Org..." wailed Jindrax.
"Don't worry, Jindrax," hissed Toxica. "We know the Master Org will return."
"The Master!" cried Jindrax. "We must find the Master."

Like rats, they scurried off into the night—to meet the Rangers yet another day....

The Rangers were proud of their victory, and together they congratulated their new champion—Cole, the Red Lion Ranger.

Taylor smiled and said, "Not bad for a rookie."